PROTECTED BY THE HITMAN

A BBW & BAD BOY ROMANCE (MEN OF RUTHLESS CORP.)

LANA LOVE

LOVE HEART BOOKS

Copyright © 2021 by Lana Love

All rights reserved.

No part of this book may be reproduced in any form or by any electronic or mechanical means, including information storage and retrieval systems, without written permission from the author, except for the use of brief quotations in a book review.

Also by Lana Love

HIS CURVY BEAUTY

Your next binge-worthy series

https://www.amazon.com/dp/B07ZSF3TW9

For even more books, visit my Amazon author page at:

https://www.amazon.com/Lana-Love/e/B078KKRB1T/

CHAPTER 1
MARLON

*I*f I had something to live for, I might care about the outcome of the next five minutes...because I might be dead in the next five minutes.

This job has gone fucking sideways. Rogue is going to hand me my ass over this, even though it's not my fault. The intel didn't say there'd be ten security personnel on site.

I clear the background noise of my mind and pay attention to what I can hear. The men around me are moving, circling in as they continue their attempt to best me.

They won't. They'll be the ones dead in five minutes.

Pushing off from the wall at my back, I lunge forward, raising my arm and firing at the men in front of me.

I fire off a series of shots in quick succession, taking out two of the ten men in front of me.

Where the fuck did they come from?

I step backward and spin so that I'm shielded by a pillar in this ornate marble lobby, trying not to wince as shots hit the pillar, sending pieces of stone and dust flying.

Fuck. Fuck. Fuck. There were supposed to be two guards, possibly three. I will be paying a special visit to my informant, to find out if this was a setup or sheer incompetence. Either way, he will not like what's coming to him.

Taking a deep breath, I crouch and spin back to face the room, aiming my gun at each of my opponents. Three more go down, my bullets doing their deadly job, but five remain. Unusually for me, my nerves are jangled. I'm usually in control, but if I can't cross this lobby within the next two minutes, the only way I'll be leaving is in a body bag. And that is un-fuck-ing-acceptable.

Back behind the pillar, I calculate the number of steps it will take to get me to the doors out of here. Ten steps, five seconds. But a lot can change in five seconds.

I stand and begin my sprint, my right arm extended and firing my gun for distraction, though I hope more of my bullets land their marks.

Four.

Three.

Tw—

Fuck.

The booming sound of an un-silenced gun going off in a small space deafens me and makes me pause, but only for a millisecond. I slide a hand inside my suit jacket, wincing when it comes back sticky with blood. I welcome the adrenaline surge, because the time it keeps the pain at bay is what will save my life.

I push through the lobby door and out into the dark night. As I dive into my waiting car and speed down the surprisingly deserted street, I finally allow myself to breathe.

And then the pain starts.

I gently touch the space to the left of my stomach, above my hit, more blood coating my fingers. Pain splinters through my body like a grenade. I grit my teeth and look down, willing myself not to faint.

Donovan Bragg is escaping me now, but he won't escape me for long. The man is a drug kingpin who's been building a crime empire in Los Angeles and, even by our standards, he's a nasty piece of work. I live a violent life, but I don't abide drugs.

I allow myself to take a careful breath as I flee this hit gone wrong, angry and disappointed about not finishing the job. My hunt for him will not end until he's not breathing, which will be sooner than he wants to believe.

∼

IT'S a cold night in Los Angeles, but I drive with my windows down and my music up. The only thing that can keep me alive is the antibiotics I have at home and my customized first aid kit. What people see in movies is true – hospitals have to report gunshot wounds, and there is no way in fucking hell I'll willingly go to a hospital.

The sound of a horn blaring alerts me that I'm drifting across lanes on the street.

Fuck.

By the grace of a God I'm not sure exists, I make it back to the place I'm currently calling home. The elevator swooshes up, the building still quiet in this cold, dark hour of the morning. My feet stumble down the hallway, eventually getting me to my door. I fumble with the key, barely able to slip it into the lock before someone steps out of the elevator. I push my door open and punch in the code to silence my alarm system. Turning to the elevator, I hope my body has enough in it to keep fighting. Failure is not an option. Tonight is not the night I want to die.

Fuck. How did they find me? Was I sloppy?

The acts of reaching for my gun and turning toward the sound is more than I can take. As much as I try to fight it, dizziness and fog overpowers me. My legs fall from under me as eyes struggle to focus, to see who is finding me like this...and I can't believe my eyes. An angel with curves appears in front of me, dressed in scrubs. Anxiety grips me. I'm supposed to be home. Where am I? Blinking slowly, I see the hallway and remind myself I'm not in the hospital. I can't go to a hospital.

If this is my last moment and this angel is my final sight, then so be it.

"Hello, Angel. I'm ready for you."

CHAPTER 2
MADDIE

After another grueling fourteen-hour shift in the ER, I need to unwind.

There's a new deadly drug making the rounds in the city. It's like the drug dealers intentionally want to kill their clientele, because the number of OD cases we've seen just this last week is more than we normally see in six months. In Los Angeles, that's something.

Today, I was in the room when time of death was called for two teens, obviously siblings with their pale green eyes and vibrant red hair. It hurts my heart in indescribable ways when we get OD cases involving teens. It's just…the pain they must feel to turn to drugs like they do, it fuels my passion to save the world. My childhood was difficult, but I managed to keep it together and stay in school, then put myself through college.

In the elevator of my building, the sudden silence reverberates through my body. All I can think about is a hot shower, a stiff drink, and my bed – in that order. This loft is a recent gift to myself, a reward for all the long hours I've put in, all the money I don't have time to spend.

As soon as I enter my hallway, the sight of a man slumping against a door, blood staining his clothing, sends me back into nurse mode. My exhaustion is profound, but I can't ignore someone so clearly in need of help.

Rushing over to him, I recognize the neighbor I barely see and who seems to keep stranger hours than I do. He's always dressed in fine suits, but he sure as hell isn't a businessman. The bulge I often see above his hip suggests he's a lot more dangerous than a businessman. He looks more like one of the criminals who show up in my ER, filled with wounds like the one he has now.

"How badly are you hurt? I'll call an ambulance."

"No!"

The look in his eyes is wild. When he reaches out and grabs my arm, his grip is more powerful than I'd expect from a man in his condition.

I look at him and sigh, his refusal confirming my suspicions, not to mention that with his jacket open, his gun is on full display. Son of a bitch. Just once, just *once*, I'd like to be wrong about how I size people up. Why couldn't he be a workaholic, like half the other men in this town?

"Angel..."

I barely hear the words as his eyes close. Seeing his key in his door, I make the decision to take care of his injuries in his home, not mine. He'll bleed out if he doesn't get immediate care, but that doesn't mean I want to take care of him in my home. My home is my sanctuary, not an ER.

Pushing his door fully open, I manage to stand him up and get him to walk into the spacious expanse of his loft. The décor is spartan and highly masculine, but no dining table. *Dammit. Where am I going to work on him?* Looking around and not seeing any good surface, I take him over to where a dining table should be, and lay him out on the hardwood floor.

After checking to make sure he's not bleeding out, I scan his home and try to guess where he'd keep a first aid kit.

Everything in here is functional and orderly. Bathroom.

Sure enough, I find a first aid kit in the cupboard underneath the sink.

Holy cow!

This is a med-grade first aid kit. Glancing back to my neighbor, I guess about his past, settling on military. With a variety of antibiotics on hand, this man is obviously experienced with wounds and treating them. *Former military?* Cephalosporin is not something the average person has.

I snap on a pair of gloves and get to work. He barely flinches as I clean his wound. Satisfied that no part of the bullet is still inside him, I stitch him up and bandage his wounds.

Leaving a patient on the floor isn't the greatest idea, but I need to get my bearings in his loft. Despite these being called lofts, they are just condos that happen to be quite large. When my real estate agent mentioned this building to me, I wondered if it would be a throwback to movies from the 1980s and 1990s. Maybe they were, back then, but now there are walls and distinct rooms.

His – I realize I don't even know this guy's name, even though I've just saved his life – loft is larger than mine and I discover three bedrooms. One bedroom looks like an office, with several locked cabinets lining two of the walls. The other two bedrooms are both Spartan and I guess that the one with the larger bed must be his.

"Hey." I speak loudly and firmly, using my stern nurse voice. "We need to move you."

It takes a few minutes, but he stands with my assistance and allows me to walk him to his bedroom.

To ensure that the sun doesn't wake him up when it rises in a few hours, I go to the window so that I can draw the curtains closed. Outside his window, there is a partially unobstructed view of hills in the distance, a faint outline of lights marking them. As I pull the curtains, my eyes scan the building across from us and I freeze when I see a man looking at me. He's standing in darkness, so still that I wonder if I'm hallucinating from exhaustion. But with the way my skin crawls, I *know* he's watching me.

But that doesn't make any sense. Unless... I finish close the curtains and then look to the now-sleeping man in the bed behind me.

Exactly who *are you?*

After he's settled in his bed, I walk around his loft, curious to get an idea of who he is, besides being a criminal. I need to go home and sleep, but I can't leave him just yet. Part of me wants to, but I need to check his vitals soon, to make sure he's stable. He may not want to go to a hospital, but there's only so much I can do.

I walk around the living room of his loft in the dark, pulling all the curtains closed before I turn on the light. My skin still crawls from having discovered someone watching me like that. Were they looking for him? Was it the man who shot this guy?

With the light on, I look around and this place is spartan by any standard. How long has he lived here? I haven't lived in this building long, but his place looks barely lived in, like it's a crash pad or a second home. There isn't anything homey about this place.

In one corner of the living room, there is a fancy leather couch against a wall, with a fancier flat-screen television on the wall opposite. Not far from the television are two bookshelves, filled with a handful of books and a few photographs. In the corner of one shelf, almost hidden, is an older-looking photo of a man with a young boy. I guess that the boy is the man whose loft I'm in, because even as a boy, he had the same green eyes and bright blond hair. Both the man and the boy aren't smiling and aren't touching, as if the photo was taken under duress.

Picking up a hardbound book that turns out to be a biography of Abraham Lincoln, I flip through the pages. I stop when I come to a page with a stiff certificate tucked between two pages. I read the Certificate of Appreciation, presented to a Marlon Snyder, presumably the man sleeping in the bedroom, for funding some project for something called the Wilderness Initiative for Boys.

"Well, that's interesting," I mutter as I slide the book back into its place, then look at the rest of the titles. Most of the books are non-fiction, but surprisingly there are also a few novels I recognize from shortlists of famous book awards. I don't know what I thought a criminal would read, but this certainly isn't it. These books make him seem more like a real person, but the variety of them has me asking even more questions.

I feel the post-adrenaline crash coming, which means it's time to check on my patient, and then go home so I can sleep. He's sleeping soundly when I return to his bedroom, one arm flung across the bed, almost as in invitation.

His vitals stable, I delicately check to make sure his wound isn't bleeding, then I take a seat by his bed and watch him. In sleep, his face looks softer and I can't deny he's the sexiest man I've ever seen. He called me an angel, but the soft light from his bedside lamp makes his blond hair glow and make *him* look like an angel. A jaw that looks professionally chiseled, long eyelashes, full lips, enviably white-blonde hair. This man could grace the cover of any magazine or lead in any movie…but that's not the life he's chosen.

~

"Who are you?"

I jump at the anger in his voice, my sleep cut short by more adrenaline flooding my body. The hair on my arms stands up and I immediately wonder if it was a mistake to help him. How could I have been so foolish as to fall asleep here? There's more than just aggression in his voice, but… something that sounds like a warning, too.

"I'm Maddie. I'm your neighbor?" I sit up straight and force myself to look into his eyes, though I'm still struggling to clear my head from the fug of sleep. The adrenaline has me alert, but my brain function hasn't caught up yet. I know how to take care of myself, but the voice in my head is very loud and clear about not messing with this guy. Most people don't end up with a gunshot wound to the gut, and fewer people will refuse to go to a hospital when they desperately need it, and even fewer people will actually have the med supplies to deal with such a wound themselves. "You were laying on the floor, half in and half out of this place. You were hurt, I'm a nurse, so I cleaned you up."

The light shifts in his green eyes and some of the taut tension in his body relaxes. He reaches to touch his torso, his eyes never leaving me, even as he flinches when his fingers graze his wound.

"I guess I should thank you. Didn't seem like I'd been hurt that much."

"Are you kidding?" I can't stop myself from laughing, even though his brow creases and it's plain as day he does not like being laughed at. "You had a gunshot wound to the gut. You're lucky it went out, instead of getting lodged in your spine or hitting a major organ. You want to tell me what happened?"

His green eyes narrow at me, his shoulders tightening. *Who is this guy?* The hair rises on my skin when I realize that *maybe* laughing at him wasn't a good idea. I remind myself that this man is *dangerous*.

"No, I'm not going to discuss what happened or why. Are you planning on reporting this?"

The gravity and challenge of his voice makes me pause. I know that I should, but not for the first time since I came home last night, fear pricks at my skin. What the hell have I gotten myself into?

I shake my head, but I can't help looking away. He's exactly the kind of man who sends people into my ER. When I turn my head back to him, his piercing eyes are watching me carefully and I know I'm being assessed.

"Look. I should go home. You're clearly doing better this morning. I worked fourteen hours in the ER and I was already exhausted." As soon as I remember the intensity of yesterday's shift at the hospital, the weight of it threatens to overwhelm me. I knew that working in the ER in Los Angeles wasn't going to be a cakewalk, but…when they tell you to prepare yourself, that's a gross understatement of the reality of what we see on a daily basis.

"Sure. Can I call you if I need help? Leave your number." While this is posed as a question, I have the distinct impression this question is more a courtesy than an actual question. He's clearly not the kind of man who gets anything less than exactly what he wants.

"Of course, though I'll be dead to the world for the next eight hours. You take it easy and take one pill daily of that antibiotic from your med kit. Oh, one more thing."

He tilts his chiseled face at me and desire punches me deep in my core. No matter that this guy is clearly bad news, my body responds to him. I know that if we saw each other in the hall under normal circumstances, he probably wouldn't look at a woman like me. Men like him only date actresses or supermodels – they don't date fat nurses.

"Shoot."

I wince, not sure if he really talks like that or if he's trying to make a joke.

"What's your name?"

CHAPTER 3
MARLON

"Snyder. What the fuck happened? Why is Bragg still alive? Why haven't you checked in before now? The client is furious." Rogue's voice booms as we talk over a secure video chat. His face is red with unsuppressed rage. I understand. Failure is not an option in this business and the clients of Ruthless pay exorbitantly for our services.

"You wanna know what happened? Bad intel fucking happened." Fury and apprehensiveness war inside of me. Of course I'm fucking angry. But Rogue is also a no-nonsense kind of guy and he doesn't give a fuck about details. He expects jobs done, on time. End of story.

"Explain."

"My contact said there would be two on the security detail. There were ten. I wasn't prepared for that." I cringe at the memory. That security detail came out of nowhere and it got real dangerous real fast. "I nearly died because my contact lied to me or didn't know what the fuck he was talking about."

"Don't make excuses." Rogue's glowering face fills my computer screen as he leans forward. "You better deal with that."

"What the *fuck*? Not my fault. Things changed or the intel was wrong. Ain't nothing I can do about that." Rogue is a hardass, but he's usually a fair man. A deep bite of pain burns through me as I turn too quickly. I clench my teeth together, not wanting Rogue to see me weak. "But yeah, I'll follow up on this. I need a few more days, though," I say, shifting again in my chair so my side doesn't brush against the arm rest.

"You don't have a few more days. Client paid to have this taken care of yesterday."

I close my eyes for a long moment. I know what the client needs and I have every intention of finishing this job, followed closely by dealing with the guy who gave me shit intel.

"Rogue. I need to heal. I can't—"

The scream is so loud, even Rogue hears it and jerks his head at the sound. It's not often that I've seen the man surprised, but he's surprised.

"The fuck is that?"

The sound of something heavy hitting the ground, followed by a familiar voice yelling. It's Maddie.

"Gotta go." I slam the screen of my laptop down, cutting off the video chat with my boss.

Rogue may be my boss, but I have to save the angel who saved me.

~

I GRAB a gun as I run toward Maddie's loft. In the hallway, I realize she didn't say which neighbor she was, but when I hear more thuds, I snap my head to the left. The door is ajar and my eyes notice the faint scratches on the deadbolt keyhole. Someone knew what they were doing.

Raising my gun, I charge into the loft. I immediately see Maddie trying to wrestle out of a man's arms.

"Back away now!" My voice booms in her loft and both she and the man freeze. Her eyes track to me, wide in terror. The man keeps his arms wrapped around her, turning so that she's between us, her body shielding him.

"You pissed off the wrong people, Babyface."

"Don't call me..." I let my voice trail off. Anyone who doesn't want their ass handed to them knows better than to call me Babyface. That means this asshole knows me or, possibly worse, has spent enough time stalking me to know my hated nickname.

Fuck.

He's not here for Maddie, he's here because of me.

"How's that baby face going to look when I kill your girlfriend here?" His voice is a sneer and my finger aches to caress the trigger and take this son of a bitch out. I want to see his face, so I can figure out who the hell is behind this. This is a problem that needs to end today.

"I told you, you fucking moron, I'm *not* his girlfriend!"

"I love it when they fight, don't you, Babyface? Makes the kill so much more fun."

The intruder moves back toward a window. The pain on Maddie's red face bothers me more than I want to admit. I haven't let anyone matter to me in more years than I can remember, but...why the hell is Maddie different?

My mind files that question away for another time.

"You hurt her and you'll have me to deal with, motherfucker." I train my gun on what I can see of his shoulder. If he doesn't move, it's a clean shot. If he moves...fuck. Maddie could die.

"Like last night?"

Tension coils in me.

"She has nothing to do with that. Or me."

"Sure, Babyface. I believe you."

In a swift move, he roughly shoves Maddie toward me. I lunge to catch her, and the intruder breaks a large window and then runs down the fire escape.

I didn't even see his face, but I'll find him. I have to find him, because this won't end until one of us is dead. And it won't be me that dies.

Maddie falls into me and I wrap my arms around her, stopping her from falling onto the hardwood floor.

Adrenaline floods my body, the urge to chase after the intruder as powerful as anything. Yet I stay back, because I need to make sure Maddie is okay. It's also flat-out stupid to chase after someone when I'm wounded like this. It'd be too easy for someone to hurt me worse, not to mention it's hard to fight well when you're not in peak condition.

"Get your arms off me!" Maddie pushes against my chest, nearly knocking me on my ass. Her blue eyes are wild with fury. "What the fuck have you gotten me into? I knew you were trouble, but no. I'm a nurse and I have to save every fucking person who needs it. Goddamn I should know better."

"I'm sorry," I say, actually meaning it. *Why do I care what she thinks?* "Do you know who that was?"

She scoffs and I walk over to the broken window. As I expected, he's long gone. Dammit. Another problem to solve.

"Maybe the guy who was staring into your loft last night?" Maddie's voice is sarcastic, but there's a tremble in it, too. She's about to crash off the adrenaline she's feeling.

"Repeat that." My skin tingles as I turn to look back at her. What the hell kind of mess has Rogue gotten me into with this assignment?

"After I cleaned your wound and stitched you up, I went to close the curtains. There was a guy in the building across the street, staring dead at me. I thought it was a coincidence."

"No, that was no coincidence. Look. Pack a bag."

"Excuse me?" Anger floods her voice. This isn't going to be easy. "Why the hell do you think I'm going to do anything you say? Thank you for just saving my life, but take your ass and your problems out of my loft and out of my life. Please and thank you!"

"It doesn't work like that." She's understandably spooked, but she's going to have to understand that she's not safe here.

"Oh, please." She stalks over to her window, a stifled cry coming from her mouth. I watch as she goes to a closet and pulls out a broom.

"Let me help."

"Don't you think you've done enough? I don't need your help."

"Yes, you do." I watch as she starts sweeping, glinting shards of glass scraping across her floor. "He's going to come back and believe me when I say it won't be good if you're here when that happens."

"I can take care of myself."

"Not with someone like him you can't."

Maddie looks at me, her eyes shifting as she looks at me. Her body starts to slump.

"Yes, I can." Realization is dawning in her eyes, but she's not giving up the fight yet. I admire her spunk. That kind of thing can get her killed, but not if I can help it.

"No. You're coming with me."

"But what about my window? What about my door?"

"I'll have one of the guys come and take care of that. In the meantime, you're coming with me and I'm going to keep you safe."

"But…" The outrage on her face is starting to fade. Without the power that adrenaline fuels, the reality that she nearly just died is hitting her and fear rises again in her eyes. The first time you look violent death in the face, it scares the fuck out of you.

"No buts. You're coming with me."

She sits heavily on her couch, fear on her face. She doesn't deserve this, but I'm not going to abandon her and leave her to fight a fight that isn't hers to begin with. Pulling my phone from my pocket, I call Rogue back.

"It's about fucking time!" Rogue's voice booms.

"Not now," I interrupt. "We have a situation. I'm bringing someone in. I need a couple of guys over here now, to secure a property. Then I'm taking Angel to Stella's."

CHAPTER 4
MADDIE

After arguing with Marlon for the entire car ride here, I'm speechless when the elevator opens onto the sleekest office I've ever seen in my life. With modern, monochromatic furniture and high ceilings, this place looks like something out of a movie. *What the hell kind of organization* is *this?*

Marlon places his hand on my lower back as we walk across the office. It feels like a betrayal when my body warms under his touch. Any other day of my life, I'd be over the moon to be in the company of such a sexy man, but the conflict from the kind of man he is spurs deep emotions in me. He's the kind of man who sends people to my ER...and that's something I can't abide. I don't even understand what it is exactly that he even does, but I know that it *is* violent and probably illegal.

"Wait here." Marlon's voice is a command and I take a seat as he goes into a glass-walled conference room and talks to an older man with scars on his face and who I'm guessing is his boss.

This place is amazing. Large, striking paintings adorn all of the exposed-brick walls. Everything about this office screams money and...danger. This is a fancy office, but there's an air about the place that's unsettling. Aside from the art, there's nothing personal to take the edge off the severity of the place. Then I realize this place is nearly empty. It's strange – like this place is for show, not to do actual work.

With the door closed, I can't hear their conversation, but I can see it. Marlon and Rogue are standing, squared off against each other. Marlon's hands flex into fists as his face flashes in anger. They come to some kind of agreement, but when they come out, his boss doesn't look pleased one bit.

"Hand over your keys."

Rogue barks out the command as if he expects me to obey him. But the look in his eyes frightens the living daylights out of me.

"Excuse me?" My voice is tiny, and I hate that I'm cowering in front of this strange man, but for all the sass I gave Marlon, it is very clear that this is not a man to talk back to.

"We're sending a team to secure your place," Marlon says. "We're going to install new locks, but it's better if we have your keys to get in."

If I didn't know better, I'd say there was something akin to an apology in Marlon's voice.

Without speaking, I reach into my purse and hand over my keys. This feels like something out of a movie – unsuspecting young nurse gets drawn into a dangerous world that she doesn't understand, and handsome man upends her life. I didn't ask for this!

"Go to Stella's and someone will call when we track Bragg."

~

"Tell me about yourself."

I look up from the Italian takeout that Marlon picked up from the place downstairs. Marlon is staring at me intently. This place looks a lot like the office – sleek and expensive, but with a lot more electronics and obvious security. Multiple deadbolts on a door that looks like solid steel, heavy curtains that look like Kevlar, locked cabinets that I'd bet a lot of money on for holding guns and weapons.

"Well, as we've established, I'm a nurse. I work in the ER." My voice snaps at him, even though I'm starting to accept the gravity of the situation.

After going to that fancy office, and then being whisked away in a dark SUV with tinted windows, and then practically sneaking into this heavily secured building, I'm realizing that Marlon maybe isn't overstating things. This organization clearly has a lot of resources.

Marlon holds his hands up in a gesture of surrender and something like hurt passes over his eyes.

"Look. I know this isn't... This isn't what you asked for. But I'm not going to let you get hurt just because you were in the wrong place at the wrong time."

"I should apologize." The more time I'm around Marlon, the more I'm rethinking how I feel about him. Clearly, he and these other guys follow rules that they define, not any laws. But there's also something about Marlon. One of the guys who showed up at the office to take my keys called him Babyface – which he wasn't pleased with at all – and it's true. He looks like he's barely out of high school, but when I look closely and watch him, I can see years of hardship etched on his face.

"No. You don't." His voice is firm as he gestures toward the box with garlic bread in it. I shake my head, indicating he should take the last piece. "But tell me about you. Where you come from."

There's a curiosity in his voice and it sounds like more than an idle question. I have a sense that he's genuinely interested, though I don't know why.

"Well," I say, taking a deep breath, "it goes something like this: difficult childhood, forced to grow up early and try to take care of my mom, ended up as a nurse because apparently my job in life is to take care of other people."

"What happened when you were a kid?"

There's an intensity and a look almost like anger in his eyes. It's weird, because I know the anger isn't directed at me. It looks more like recognition of a shared experience and it makes me wonder what his story is.

I close my eyes for a long moment. The truth is I try not to think about the past, even though I can't escape the way it shaped who I am.

"Dad got involved with some lowlife criminals. Got involved in drugs, ended up getting killed. Mom fell apart and never got it back together. That happened when I was in middle school. It was either step up and take care of my mom and me, or end up in the foster system."

Tears prick at my eyes. Even though it's been years since then, and my mom is gone now, it still hurts to remember that time. I catch my emotions and push them back down, not wanting to reveal just how much my past still has a hold on my life.

"Anyway. It's a boring story." I close the box of chicken alfredo and push it away from me. "What's your story? Or can I ask?"

"You can ask. It's not that different than yours, really. I grew up with my dad. Mom left when I was four. Dad resented that Mom left, so he took it out on me."

Marlon winces almost imperceptibly as he talks, showing the depth of his emotion about this. I don't interrupt him.

"Dad was a hard man."

"What happened to him?"

"Life in prison. Haven't seen him since I was eighteen." Marlon rubs his hand over his face, then stares out the window.

Jealousy washes over me, then I realize maybe I don't have anything to be jealous about. Yes, his father is still alive, but it's not like they have the possibility of a good relationship.

Still, it's hard not to be jealous. It's more like feeling jealous of the *possibility*, of maybe being able to have something resembling a positive relationship with his father. Though I also know, from my experience with my mom, that all the love and all the effort in the world can't fix some relationships.

"I'm sorry." I'm never sure what to say in situations like this.

"Don't be. I'm not. Man is a fucking asshole."

I jerk back at the venom in his voice. The light in his eyes goes dark and I let the subject drop.

"About the last twenty-four hours."

"What about them?" It's a stupid question to ask, because from the intensity of how he's looking at me and how his body is radiating tension right now, I can't help but shiver as I sit across from him. I already know I'm not going to like what he's going to say.

"If you haven't already figured it out, there is some serious shit going down. You can't go home. You can't go to work."

"Wait a minute!" I thought I was going to get a speech on personal safety and locking doors and having a security system installed. Being told that my life was on hold never crossed my mind. "People are depending on me!"

"If you value your life – and I hope you do – you can't go back."

I collapse onto the couch, wanting to fight, but realizing it's useless. The look on Marlon's face is one of absolute seriousness, not jest.

"I just bought that place." My chest heaves. "For too long, I've been unwilling to settle down anywhere, to commit to anything. I thought, *OK,*

*Mads, time to grow up and make a home...*and look where it got me. Maybe this is the universe's way of telling me not to settle down."

"It's just a loft."

"Just a loft?" I jerk away from Marlon when he touches me. How can he sound so dismissive about my home? I don't care if I haven't lived there very long or that I still have unpacked boxes – it's my *home*.

"Yes, it is. There are other lofts and houses. I don't say this to be cruel. After..." Marlon pauses, his face filling with emotion. "I've led an itinerant life, but I'd be lying if I said I hadn't dreamed of having a home, a place I wanted to return to, a place that I might one day have a family – even though a family is the last thing most men like me have or even deserve."

"After what?"

"After the life I've had, I know that homes are only reflections of the people in them. You can put your things anywhere."

"You may not mean that to sound cruel, but it is."

Marlon looks at me, exasperation written all over his face.

"What the fuck did you think was happening when you saved my life? You cleaned up a gunshot wound!"

"I..." My voice trails off. Of course, he's right. The remains of so much violence comes through the ER, that even though I know how it happens, I sometimes try to block out the specifics of it. Like if I don't think about who sent people to me, that maybe that means the world isn't as bad as it really is. *Be brave, Maddie, but don't be naive.* "Then why don't you tell me what happened and what's going on?"

The unexpected force in my voice seems to take Marlon by surprise. He leans back in his chair, running his hand across his torso and wincing when he reaches the area that I patched up for him. Was it really just last night?

"These are men that you don't want to be involved with."

"Please," I say, drawing the word into two long syllables. "I'm involved. I saved you and apparently now they're coming after me. Don't I have a right to know?"

Marlon lowers his eyes from mine, taking a deep breath as he looks across the room, toward the windows that have heavy curtains drawn. After a long moment, he nods and returns his gaze to me.

"I'll be blunt. But first, I'll strongly advise you to keep all of this information to yourself. Not only will I deny everything, but you'll have a whole new group of men hunting you. Rogue will have your ass if you spill any of this to anyone, especially the police or the press. Are we clear?"

Fear wells up in me. What the hell did I stumble into? They say that you never know when you reach that moment that changes your life, but for me it was when I saw Marlon on the floor and helped him. If I hadn't pulled a shift with overtime, if he had made it fully into his loft, I wouldn't have found him and we wouldn't be sitting here right now. I wouldn't be about to hear all the drastic and dramatic ways my life was changing.

"Yes. You're very clear."

"Good. I'm a hitman."

"You're what?" My voice screeches out of me. I mean, I didn't think this guy was a teacher, but this is way beyond what I thought.

"Exactly as I said. Rogue gets assignments, and then we go out and eliminate the targets."

"But... Who do you kill? Who makes that decision?"

"Client gives us a name, they pay the money, we do the job. Simple as that." Marlon looks at me like he's stating the obvious. "If it makes you feel better, every target deserves it. No," he holds up his hand and closes his eyes for a long second, "don't tell me our targets don't deserve it. They do. Imagine the most dangerous men you've heard about...then imagine men far worse than them. There is no mistake about them having earned a visit from one of us."

My mind races, already filling with so many questions. I'm not sure I want to know, but I realize that I need to know. If I'm in the middle of this, then I need to know exactly what I'm in the middle of. Clasping my hands together, to try and hide how they're shaking, I look Marlon straight in the eye. "Tell me exactly what's going on."

Marlon tells me a story that sounds like something out of a movie. He was supposed to take out a crime lord, but things didn't go as planned. He ended up with a gunshot wound, the target, as he called him, escaped. When he begins explaining who Donovan Bragg is, I hold up my hand.

"I know who he is." Anger laces my voice and I don't try to hide it. I'm pretty sure that man's cartel or whatever it's called is what led to my father's death. I know my father made his own choices and chose to break the law, but it's men like Bragg who prey on the weak and exploit their needs. "But how does he know who *I* am? That doesn't make sense."

"You said you saw someone when you were at the window, right? That means they saw you. Don't underestimate how fast and thoroughly someone with the right tools at their disposal can unearth the information they want."

"So…" I struggle to say the words, but I have to ask the question. "Are you going to finish the job? Are you going to…kill," I say the word quietly, "Donovan Bragg?"

"Of course I am. I have to finish the job." There isn't any hesitation in his voice. It's like asking someone if they want pizza for dinner.

Sitting across from Marlon, my mind shifts in the way I see him. I saved him, then he saved me, and now he's going to kill someone. He's going to *assassinate* them.

I wrap my arms around myself as my body starts shaking uncontrollably. It's like my mind thought this was all an abstract conversation, and then it realized it was real. Marlon kills people for a living. Someone tried to kill me, just because I helped him. *My life will never be the same!*

"What does this mean for me?" My voice warbles as I ask the question. I wish I could hide how scared I've become, but I can't. "Will I ever be able to go home? Will I ever feel safe again? What about my job? I have a shift tonight."

"Like I said, you can't go home. Not soon. Maybe not ever. You also can't go to work."

"What do you mean? It's *my job*!" I sob as each wave of realizations hit me. What is happening? How will I rebuild everything I've just lost? How far do I have to move? It's not like I haven't thought about leaving L.A. before, but…not like this. Is it even possible to outrun this kind of trouble?

All at once, it hits me just how close I came to possibly dying. Shit. If they think I'm related to Marlon somehow, they weren't going to stop at asking me questions.

Adrenaline surges through my body, making my skin tingle and my heart pound. I look at Marlon, this sexy-as-sin man, and I know all the reasons I should hate him. I hate the vigilante justice that he stands for. But this man saved my life. He didn't have to, but he did.

"Thank you." I rush over to him and wrap my arms around him, desperately needing to feel the touch of another human being. At first, his body is stiff in my arms, then he exhales.

Marlon wraps his strong arms around me and pulls me even closer to his body. His voice is husky and uneven when he speaks.

"This is dangerous."

When I start to pull away, he doesn't release my body. A flash of alarm ricochets through my mind, then I look at his face. His eyes are filled with a fierce hunger and, in that moment, no matter how much I hate what he stands for, I don't care.

"Kiss me." At first, I'm not sure if I actually spoke the words or if he heard me. But then his hands move down my back and cup my ass, and he lowers his mouth to mine.

His mouth is demanding, and I thrust my body against his, hungry for everything that I want to happen.

"This is dangerous." He repeats himself, but his hands are sliding under my shirt, his fingers hot and probing against my bare skin. Each stroke of his fingers sends my heart racing faster and faster. I lower one of my hands and hook my finger under the waistband of his jeans. His skin contracts under my touch and I stroke him, relishing how he squirms under my touch.

"I have you to protect me."

"But who will protect you from me?"

I look into his eyes and fumble with the buttons of his jeans. I need Marlon in a way I've never needed anyone else. After what's happened, I need to feel alive again. I need to *feel*. "I don't need protecting from you."

He lets go of me and pulls his shirt over his head and I do the same. I don't even bother to try and suck in my stomach. I don't even think of it. Right now, my needs are primal and urgent, and I simply don't care about anything else.

"You need protecting from me."

"What I need is for you to fuck me."

CHAPTER 5
MARLON

*E*verything about this is wrong, but I can't stop. Maddie in my arms is the best thing I've felt in I don't know how long. She has the body of a woman and a passion to match.

I lead her into the bedroom, my mind fogged with lust. I need to see her body, to spread those sweet, thick thighs of her, then plunge my cock into her sweet pussy.

We make it to the bed and she giggles as it hits the back of her knees. Watching her big tits jiggle as she climbs into bed makes my cock hard as steel and ache to be free. She sits up, her hands going back to my jeans.

A guttural moan escapes me as she pushes my jeans down and my cock springs free.

"You're beautiful." Her voice is a breathy gasp and I nearly come when I see her lick her lips and open her mouth.

"Fuck. You're hot."

Her tongue flicks out of her mouth, pink and teasing of pleasure.

"Face, we gotta go. They found Bragg."

Carter barges into the bedroom, not even looking twice at Maddie and me, which is good. If he stared at her, I might have to kill him. We haven't even fucked, but she's mine.

"Fuck." Frustration hits me like a truck. But I know that I have to take care of this. I have to complete the job and, more importantly, I have to protect Maddie. Losing her is not, and will never be, an option.

"Maddie," I say quietly, holding her jaw in my hands. "I have to take care of this. It's important that you stay here. Don't move. No going to the window, no opening the door, no phone calls. There's a tv in the living room. I need you to stay safe."

She must recognize what I'm feeling, because she bites her lip and nods. Maddie puts her hand above the wound she stitched up, and looks me in the eye.

"Be safe. I want to see you come through that door in one piece. I will if you need it, but I'd prefer not to patch up another gunshot wound. Okay?"

I pull her into my arms and give her a hard, fast kiss. It's nowhere near enough, but it's all we have time for.

"I'll be back for you soon."

∼

I DON'T OBJECT to Carter going with me. In other circumstances, Rogue instructing him to join me would be a signal that he thinks I'm weak or incompetent. As much as I don't want to admit it, tonight I do need help. I'm still hurting from the gunshot wound, plus after the failure last night, he'll know I'm coming and will guaranteed have more hired guns surrounding him.

"They know we're coming." I say this as a statement. There's no way they can't. Maybe they don't know we're speeding down the Los Angeles freeway at this very moment, but he now knows there's an active target on his back and that, if not me, *someone* is coming to finish what I failed to last night.

"They're not stupid." Carter's voice is curt, his eyes focused on the road as we speed toward the warehouse that we tracked Bragg to. "You okay to finish the job? You better not be distracted."

I glare at Carter when we get to a stoplight and he stares at me. He's wrong about Maddie – she's not a distraction, she's giving me purpose.

"I'll be fine. We're going in, hot and fast. *You* better not slow me down."

Carter grunts in response and he drives the rest of the way in silence. I check my guns, then meditate to clear my mind before we get there. There's nothing more in the world right now than my absolute desire to be with Maddie. Being with Maddie has lifted me up from a fog that I didn't even know I'd been living in. I've been a hitman because it's something I'm good at, but also because I had nothing to lose.

Now, I have Maddie to lose. I can't let her down and sure as the sun rises in the east, I will make it back to her. She holds the promise of a future that means something.

∼

"KILLING ME ISN'T GOING to stop this." The man with my gun pressed to his neck challenges me, his voice filled with bravado or stupidity. Fool thinks he can talk his way out of this. He's a job, for which my bank account will become fatter. "If you think—"

I shut him up with a bullet to the brain. Just like I did his security detail, including the guy who attacked my Angel. Moment he opened his mouth, I knew who he was. He didn't finish his sentence before a bullet from my gun ricocheted through his skull.

Tapping my ear piece, I untwist the silencer on the gun as I call Rogue.

"Status?" Rogue's voice is a bark.

"Job complete. Send cleanup." Sometimes you leave the body behind as a statement, sometimes you disappear the body to make another statement. Client wants the body disposed of, so that's what will happen. There ain't going to be any mistake about what happened to Bragg, but the client wants the body disposed of, so dispose of the body is what we will do.

Rogue terminates the connection and I take a seat as I wait. I rest my hand on my lap, my fingers still wrapped around my gun. Despite Carter standing guard by the front door to this place, it doesn't mean more trouble isn't coming.

Even though I didn't let the guy talk, I know he's right. This job was complicated when I didn't terminate him the first time and his team clearly know who I am. Fuck. They know who Maddie is, too.

Maddie. My Angel.

I wish she wasn't involved in this, but without her I'd probably be dead. Fuck. It's been a long time since I was willingly vulnerable with another person and having her see me when I was at my most vulnerable? It stirs a lot of feelings. She's clearly not pleased with the life I lead, but...I find myself wanting...no, *needing*...to win her over and for more than something like the hot fuck that got interrupted.

"Yo, Face." The boom of Carter's voice snaps me back to the present moment. As I stand up, my gut throbs, reminding me of my wound. I need to get back to Maddie and have her look at this.

I walk out to the floor of the warehouse, motioning the cleaners to the office behind me.

My job done, I'm ready to get back to Maddie.

∽

"Yo, Face. Have you told her yet?" Carter asks when we're at a stoplight. This is an industrial area and the streets out here are quiet, but you always take special care after a job, because the last thing you need is a cop looking to fill a quota.

"Told her what?"

"That she can't go back. Neither can you, at least not to live there. You know that. If they know where you live, that news is going down the grapevine as we speak. You know it."

I do know this. Maddie was furious.

"I've been trying to ignore how that conversation went." I hit the steering wheel lightly with my palm, frustration putting me on edge. "If Stella's wasn't soundproofed, you'd have heard the yelling."

I've made it a point to not have ties I couldn't break, to not have people I cared too deeply for, because I know everything is temporary. I also know far too well how temporary life is and how easy it is to slip in like the night and take a life. That's a constant threat in my life and I'm not enough of an asshole to share that grim reality with another person, let alone a woman.

"Good luck with that." Carter barks a laugh and I understand completely. Maddie is a fighter.

CHAPTER 6
MADDIE

All my life, I've taken care of other people. At first, it was an obligation, because I had to keep it together as I tried to look out for my mom, even though she berated me for looking out for her. Somehow being a caretaker stuck. I've felt resentful at times, for not having anyone to look after me and not being able to have fun like the other girls in school, but caring for people is the heart of who I am. When I was a teenager, I fantasized that the moment I was eighteen, I'd move out of the apartment and then go wild.

Instead, I ended up going first to community college and then to nursing school. Once I was on my own, I vowed on my life never to let anyone who hurt or took advantage of others into my life. Every day, I see the damage that comes from the violence and neglect of other people. People think working in Los Angeles is glamorous and that movie stars are my patients, but…no. I work in a public hospital. The people who need our help are people who remind me of my parents and what might have happened to me if I hadn't stayed in school.

I've defined my life by helping other people. Marlon takes life from other people. That's just… I turn off the television and throw the remote on the sofa. This isn't a normal day off from work, where sleeping all day or watching mindless television would be a nice way to pass the time.

There's at least one strange man in my loft, fixing the damage and, if the looks of this safehouse are any indication, means that if and when I can go home, that I'll be going home to Fort Knox. Then there's me getting sexy and somehow falling for my neighbor the hitman.

When I realize I'm reaching for the curtain, so I can open the window for what passes for fresh air here in L.A., I freeze. I'm not naïve enough to think that Marlon was exaggerating about the danger level right now. They didn't even try to hide the guns they had.

I pace around the living room, fighting the urge to bolt, even though I have no idea where I'd go and that I think I'm locked in here. Part of me doesn't even want to go, because of what I've been feeling for Marlon. It's only been a day, but what I feel isn't just lust and I don't think the attraction is just based on shared adverse experience. As much as I try to fight it or explain it away, there's something about Marlon that just...it's like my heart recognizes its missing piece in him.

They say you can't control who your heart falls in love with, but... dammit, why'd I have to fall in love with a criminal?

∽

"OH!" Adrenaline punches through me and my head snaps up. Blinking quickly, I see Marlon sitting next to me on the couch. "What happened?"

"You fell asleep. I didn't mean to startle you."

"Oh." I rub my hand over my face, trying to orient myself. "Everything okay? Did everything, um, go well today?"

There's a voice in my head, urging me to ask the question. But I also don't want to know. I know if his answer is yes, then that means at least one person died today, probably by Marlon. He said before that the people who are their targets aren't innocents and that they've done something to earn a visit from Marlon or the guys he works with. But…vigilante justice…it isn't justice. That's not how things are supposed to work.

"With work, yes." Marlon's voice is curt. "And yes, the target was taken care of, as was the man who attacked you yesterday."

My stomach lurches as the meaning of this sinks in. Marlon killed a man. Men. Including the man who busted into my loft and threatened me.

"I… Thank you. I think." Relief tickles me, making me wonder if maybe I can go home, if maybe my life will return to normal.

"You *think*?" Marlon's voice is sharp and I can't meet his eyes. I don't know how to explain how I feel gratitude and revulsion. It's a weird emotional cocktail.

"Look. If it hasn't been clear to you. I save lives. Nurses and doctors don't get to choose whose lives we save. We treat everyone the same – it's part of the basic job description."

"I don't understand. I thought you'd be…at the very least relieved." Something like pain flashes across Marlon's green eyes.

"Yes, I am relieved. I hate myself for feeling good that someone is dead, but I do."

I adjust myself on the couch, pulling my legs underneath me and wrapping my arms around my torso. A deep chill radiates through me, which has nothing to do with the weather.

"This is who I am."

"I know!" I reach out and touch his arm, as much to comfort him as to comfort myself.

"Carter! You need to finish up. We need some privacy."

"Yeah, yeah." The guy sighs dramatically, though when he glances toward us, I can see relief in his eyes. "I'll be down the hall."

"Good." Marlon turns to me, his eyes more open now. "Maddie, we need to talk."

~

"This doesn't mean you can go back to your loft. Or, more precisely, if you value your life, you won't." He's moving around the kitchen with an ease that says he knows this place well. He pulls a bottle of tequila and two glasses from a cupboard, then comes to me and pours a large shot. "Lime?"

"No, that's okay." I look at Marlon, speechless. The tequila burns as it goes down, but the warmth that comes from it is welcome. My mind is still screaming, but already the tequila is blurring my anger. All I know is that my life is forever changed.

I hold out my glass and Marlon refills it, but this time I sip at it.

"Then...then what's next?" I finally say, my voice small. Just like that, the fire goes out of me and I feel like a little kid being told they're permanently grounded. It's not like I haven't moved before, but I've always been the one to choose that. Right here, right now, it feels like my choice has been taken away from me. My emotions swing between fear and anger. Ever since I saved Marlon's life, the hits keep coming.

"Whatever you want to happen is next. If you could do anything, what would you do?"

"I'm not sure." I shrug, then look away from Marlon. Everything about him – his profession, his beauty, his unexpected caring and kindness for me – throws me off balance. I keep expecting him to snap at me or yell, but he never does. More than anything, I want to be with *him*. He's the first man I've ever wanted to truly let into my life. "I've thought about doing aid work. See the world, save people in far-off places."

"I know this isn't what you want to hear, but that's not a bad choice." Marlon drains his tequila and I get distracted by watching the way his muscles shift as he moves. How can a man so sexy seem so invested in who

I am and what I want? He could do anything he wanted with looks like that…but instead he kills people? I remember what he said about his childhood and realize that he was probably never going to have a "normal" life.

"If it wasn't for you, this wouldn't be happening to me!" I can't help from yelling at him. My emotions suddenly shift back to anger and I can't control my outburst. One moment I'm calm, the next my emotions are exploding like a landmine. I've always been a peacekeeper, the one keeping things together in a bad situation – but nothing in my life has prepared me for this.

"It's okay to be mad."

I look at Marlon, ready to yell at him for patronizing me, but he looks pained. Stunned, I try and take this in. Pushing aside my emotions, because they are too big for me right now, I try to focus on practicalities.

"What's next? Will I ever be safe?" My fingers pick at my t-shirt. I pull at a loose thread, watching as the hem comes undone.

"You will, yes. Especially if you let me protect you. You don't have to do this alone. I need you."

CHAPTER 7
MARLON

I've never needed someone in my life even half as much as I want and need Maddie in mine.

I just don't know if I can convince her to stay with me.

"I'm sorry, Marlon. This..." Maddie waves her hand between the two of us, tears filling her eyes. "I don't know what this is. There's no denying there's something between us, but...we're too different."

Maddie's words cut through me like a saber.

"It's...it's not like that."

"How isn't it like that?" Color flares in her cheeks, her blue eyes wide with fury. "Because from where I'm sitting, you and that other guy just went and killed at least two men, and I'm guessing more. *I am not okay with that!*"

"But I just saved your – my – life! They would have kept coming and coming. I know how they are. I am exactly the same way."

"And I appreciate that, I do." Her voice breaks and even I recognize how embarrassed she is right now. "But...I can't."

"Why not?"

She looks at me.

"I couldn't stand to be abandoned." Her voice is tiny and it scares me. I wish I didn't understand the look of pain in her eyes, but I do. The feeling of abandonment is one I know all too well.

"I get it. I told you about my dad."

"Do you really?" Her voice is sharp, but there is profound sadness in her voice, too. "You're some kind of lone wolf, killing the bad guys and not thinking twice about doing so."

I close my eyes for a long moment. There's a reason I don't talk about my past. Fuck. I try not to even think about my past.

"Have you ever wondered how someone comes to a life like I have?"

Maddie pauses and stares at me, her eyes eventually grasping what I mean.

I look away from Maddie, sorely tempted to change the subject. But if anything is going to happen between us – and by God I want it to – then she has to know and understand who I really am. "My father rode my ass hard and by any standards was an abusive motherfucker. The only useful things I learned from him were how to fight and shoot. This is all that I'm good at."

Pain creases Maddie's face and I hate that I make her feel this way.

"I'm so sorry." Her voice is soft as she reaches over and touches my arm.

It feels incredibly intimate for her to be touching me right now, more so than if we were in bed making love. Normally I'd do anything not to talk about myself or my father, but...I want her to know. I need her to know who I am, so I can know that she accepts me.

"It's the past. I haven't truly cared about another human being in years, but...Maddie, you have changed all that."

"Me?" Her blue eyes look at me with surprise.

"It's... It's hard to explain. Maybe it's because you saved my life." I reach down and touch the bandage covering the wound she cleaned for me. "Maybe it's just because in you, I see the opposite of me. You turned your hurt into something good – you save people's lives. Despite everything you've experienced, you haven't lost your heart and humanity. I've let hatred and pain fuel my decisions for too long. When I'm with you, I see the possibility of being something greater, of being a man that is more than a killer."

The look in Maddie's blue eyes tells me that she doesn't believe me. Hell, I wouldn't believe me either, and she knows nearly nothing about me. To her, what I do is whatever she imagines based on television and movies, and the people she's seen in the ER. She doesn't know about how you become cold to killing, how a target is just an item on the to-do list, like getting a haircut or getting new tires for a car. Some jobs are more complicated than others, but the gravity of taking a person's life does not affect me in the slightest.

And this is something that has bothered me, though I've done my best not to think about it. Because if I don't do this, what do I do? I don't know how to do anything else.

"Look, I appreciate that you have a conscience or at least some introspection going on, but let's be real." Maddie crosses her arms over her chest and I see her mentally disengaging. "You are who you are and I am who I am – and we're two diametrically opposed types of people. Marlon, do you really think this could work? We're too different."

I move closer to her and take her hands in mine. Her eyes are fixed on mine. As uncomfortable as it is to look her in the eyes, I do it and don't break my gaze from her.

"What if I'm willing to change? What if I *want* to change?"

"Marlon, please." Her voice is gentle as she tries to pull her hands from mine. She jumps at the sound of sirens passing the building and I wrap my arms around her, needing to protect her and shield her from her fear.

"Please," I say, my voice taking on a desperate quality that is alien to me. "Maddie, give me a chance. I already know how I feel about you. I'm ready to give my life to you. It's obvious there's something between us, right? Can you agree on that?"

"I... Yes. But...that's just lust. That's just...whatever it is they call it, when two people come together in an extreme situation. That doesn't last. It's not the foundation for love."

"What if it is? Can you just give me a chance? Give me six months? Let me prove to you that I'm the man you need, the man that I want to be."

Maddie looks at me, her eyes filled with emotion. I can tell that I have a chance, but it's also obvious that if I say or do the wrong thing, she'll be gone forever. The depth of my need for Maddie is greater than anything I've ever experienced. She is the integral piece of my life that I didn't realize was missing.

"Maddie, please."

"Are you ready to promise me you won't leave me?"

"On my life. I promise you on my life, Maddie."

"I... I want you, too, Marlon. I just can't take giving my heart to someone and then losing them – and that includes losing someone because they die."

"Maddie, I will find a new line of work. I swear to you. It's not possible to love another human being the way I love you, and then keep doing this. You have to be able to compartmentalize to do this job, but...that's a level of compartmentalizing that I'm not at. I don't want to be able to do that."

Maddie's eyes soften and she strokes my jaw, and in that moment, everything falls into place. I have no fucking idea what I'll do for work. But I can figure that out later and with Maddie.

"I need to kiss you."

"I need for you to kiss me, too." Maddie's cheeks flame in a blush and my cock comes to attention in my pants. Seeing her walls start to come down makes the wall around my heart start to crumble, and it's a scary emotion. Pulling Maddie close to me, I give into that emotion, helpless at the connection I feel for her.

The air around us burns as our kiss deepens and I weave my fingers through Maddie's dark hair.

"You are going to be the most satisfied wife this world has ever seen."

"Wife?" Maddie gasps, a smile playing on her luscious lips. "Isn't that a bit premature? Do you realize what you're saying?"

"I've been sure about you since the moment I laid eyes on you and thought you were an angel." I stand up and extend my hand to her. When she's standing in front of me, I wrap my arms around her, all my emotions transferring to her with the force of my hug. Lowering my face, I breathe in her scent as I listen to her sighs of pleasure from each kiss I place on her neck and jaw. "I'm never letting you go."

"Then I will make sure you're most satisfied husband the world has seen. Now kiss me like you mean it."

CHAPTER 8
MADDIE

"Is Carter going to come back?"

We're standing in the bedroom, our clothes piling up on the floor, our hands urgently caressing each other's skin.

"If he wants to live to see tomorrow, he won't." While Marlon smiles as he says this, I catch a current of seriousness in his voice. Having a man feel so protective of me is new to me. It makes me feel loved and valued in a way I never have been before. Looking into Marlon's eyes, I'm more confident about him than I've been about anything.

"Don't ever leave me," I whisper, wrapping my arms around Marlon and holding him tightly.

Marlon's breath catches and he hugs me fiercely. "I'll never abandon you. I'm not that stupid. I love you too much."

"But…" I pull away from him, needing to look in his eyes, "but what about your job? It scares me that there could be a day you don't come home, or that you come home with a wound that I can't treat. What then?"

Saying the words scares me. I've known enough women who tried to change their man and I know it never works, especially when you're talking about a man's career. Men define themselves by their jobs and I know you can't ask a man to change that.

"I've thought about this." Marlon's voice is serious. He doesn't try to look away. "I'm ready to leave this life. I know a guy who does security – corporate shit, tough-guy-in-suit shit – I can do that. Before you, Maddie, I didn't have a reason to do anything different. The possibility of dying wasn't something that scared me. But now," he cups my face with his hands, then lowers his mouth to mine in a firm kiss, "you give me a reason to want to live. With you, I want to come home at the end of the day, I want to sleep in your arms, I want to raise a family with you."

The gravity of what he's saying takes my breath away. He's willing to compromise.

"You would put me…us…first like that?" The hole in my heart that I've felt since my mom neglected me, it feels like that hole is being erased by Marlon's love. The sense of feeling like I wasn't good enough to devote to, Marlon makes me realize that I am good enough, that he sees the value in me and will honor me in the way I've been too scared to hope that anyone would ever do.

"Of fucking course I would and I will. You mean everything to me, Maddie."

Marlon's voice hitches and he kisses me again. This time, his kiss is deep and probing. He weaves his fingers through my hair and tilts my head back, and I give myself over to him. I moan into his mouth, my tongue stroking his, hungry to taste all of him.

We pause long enough to remove the rest of our clothes and I nearly cry when I see the look in his eyes as he looks at me. He bites his lip, as if he's looking at something that takes his breath away.

"You're a fucking angel. You're so beautiful." Marlon reaches out and I shiver as his fingers trace over my skin. He takes his time as he touches me and it makes me want him even more. With Marlon, there's no wanting to

PROTECTED BY THE HITMAN

hide in the dark, no wondering if he's going to fuck and run, he's just...I know he's here, with me, because he wants me. He wants me as his wife. I want him as my husband.

This isn't just something we're getting out of our system after being in mortal danger. What's between us is the beginning of forever.

I pull Marlon close to me, being careful not to bump his wound.

"Don't worry about me. I can take it," he says, his eyes following my hand.

I laugh a little, but shake my head. "You may think you can, but as your nurse, I say you shouldn't. Lie down on the bed."

"I want you under me," he says, his voice lowering and powerful.

"Not tonight." I shake my head, gently pushing him toward the bed. "I don't want your wound to open up. There's only so much I can do outside a hospital. No, don't protest," I put my finger up to his mouth, a sound of surprise escaping my lips as he nips at my fingertip and his tongue flicks against my skin. "There's enough time in the world for us to try all the positions in the world. Tonight, lay back."

The light changes in Marlon's green eyes, and then a smile lifts his lips.

"I like this side of you."

In bed, I carefully straddle his hips, shivering with pleasure when his thick member bumps against my core. Gently, I rub myself over him, satisfaction rushing over me as Marlon groans and presses his hips up into me.

"You like this?" I rock my hips over him, my body craving him. We need to finish what we started, to feel the release that we both need after the past few days. Saving Marlon changed my life. We can't go back, maybe not even to collect our things, but we're going forward to create something new, together. And that begins with us making love.

Marlon's hands move between my breasts and my hips as I rock my body over him, each rock of my hips taking him deeper inside of me. He's thick and long, but he fills me up perfectly and I love how my body is stretching to take more of him in.

I can see the war in Marlon's eyes as our bodies move faster and faster. It's clear that he wants to flip me over, but I put my hand on his chest to remind him, *not tonight.* I want my man healthy.

He grips my hips as he pushes his cock deeply into me, his breathing jagged as he moans my name. I take his hands and lace my fingers through his, using them to steady me as my orgasm rises from deep within me and my body moves faster and wilder.

"Come with me," I moan, grinding my hips over his. I can't get enough of him and I'm already seeing stars in front of my eyes. I'm about to explode in happiness. "I can't wait any longer."

"Then come for me, my angel."

The fire in Marlon's eyes sends me over the edge and I buck and grind against him, taking every bit of him inside of me. My core expands and then explodes, pleasure bursting in every cell of my body. Beneath me, Marlon's body bucks and a wild look fills his eyes as he grips my hips again, keeping me steady as he calls out my name and comes with me.

"It's not going to be like this all the time," he says, when his breathing has evened out and I'm lying next to him, my fingers stroking his skin.

"How do you mean?"

"First," he says, bringing my fingers to his mouth and kissing each fingertip, "it will last longer. Second," he says, again taking my fingers in his mouth and sucking on them, "I will be in charge."

My breath catches as he lowers his mouth to my breasts and wraps his lips around my nipples. A fresh wave of desire is already building in me and I'm already to make love to Marlon again. In a swift move, he moves his body above mine and pins my arms above my head. I narrow my eyes at him, but can't help from laughing.

I'm deliciously exposed under Marlon, but it makes me happier than I've ever felt. There is nothing to hide from him. I can be who I am and I'm not worried about what he'll think of me or my past. I trust Marlon and I can't wait to see where our life leads us.

"I love you so much, Marlon."

"I love you, too, my angel."

EPILOGUE

"Take one pill per day, then come back in two weeks. Okay?" I look to the translator as she tells my patient what I've just said. The patient looks at me and smiles as she nods, relief written all over her face.

This last patient taken care of, I clean up my work area, and then take a supply inventory. As usual, the supply truck is several days late, which means we have to ration meds. Out here, schedules are based on hopes, not reliability.

"Any update on supplies?" I call out to Doctor Solano, the lead doctor of our field clinic out here in the wilds of Eastern Europe.

Solano sighs. "About as you expect. The truck should be here tomorrow, though. I got confirmation that they're on their way. But...you know how it is. You want the ultrasound?"

Solano knows what's going on, because I had to request a test, since I can't just go to the local drugstore and buy one myself. But with the supply truck delayed yet again, I touch the wedding ring I keep on a chain around my neck, then nod my head. I have to know.

When he confirms what I've suspected the last few weeks, elation surges through me. I want to sing and dance and scream from the rooftops, but most of all, I want to share this news with Marlon. I'm so excited to make him a dad and to start building our family together.

"I take it you're pleased with the results," Solano says, wiping the ultrasound gel off my stomach. "I've never seen you look this happy before."

"Yeah, even with my husband here, it's…a tough place." I touch the wedding ring around my neck. I wear it on a chain and hidden under my clothes, one to protect it from getting lost or damaged while working, and also to hide it from potential thieves. Wearing it again is something that also excites me, though I'm guessing it'll end up around my neck at some point during my pregnancy when my fingers swell up.

"It is, Maddie. It is. Of course, I'm thrilled for you," he says, pushing the ultrasound cart toward the exam room door, "but we're going to miss both of you, deeply. You've both been incredible assets to our team here."

"I'll miss you and the work here, too, but…" I splay my fingers protectively over my stomach. "It's time to go home."

∽

AFTER WHAT HAPPENED in Los Angeles, Marlon and I both agreed that we needed a change of scenery, not to mention he wanted a change after telling Rogue he was done with being a hitman for hire. Rogue wasn't pleased, but he didn't try to change Marlon's or my mind. Now, Marlon has started his own security firm and is providing security for the medical camp I'm working at this year.

"You finished up?" Marlon wraps his arms around me and I turn to hug him. We may be close to a warzone, but I feel safe with Marlon and his team protecting us.

"I am." I kiss Marlon and every nerve ending in my body wakes up. No matter how intense work is, Marlon has a magic that lights up my body and soul like nothing else. In the darkness of my work, he is my beacon of light and love. He is my guardian angel.

"Good. I've got food in the Jeep. I'll cook dinner tonight."

I arch my eyebrow at Marlon. Cooking is a new hobby for him. He's definitely getting better, but there were some...misfires early on. I love that he pampers me, especially on the difficult days that we get out here, like when there isn't medication or we don't have the equipment to help someone or we don't have the resources to move someone to a proper hospital with more resources.

This work can be grueling emotionally. Yet every day we are saving people's lives, so we shoulder the burden of this job. We work to help these people who have been abandoned by so many others.

Every day I'm thankful that Marlon agreed to do this with me. Leaving Ruthless Corp. and Rogue was a hard transition for Marlon, even though he was ready to do it. Starting his own security firm was a natural choice for him. He can leverage his strengths, without living in the darker headspace.

~

"Your contract is almost up, sweetheart. What are you thinking? Stay here? Or do you want to head further east, like you mentioned a couple months ago?"

Marlon gestures toward the kebabs, but I shake my head and push the plate toward him so he can take the last one. I've already had enough and I've found that I get queasy if I eat too much right now.

"Well," I reach over and grab his hands, "let's talk about that. Let's go sit in the other room. We'll take care of the dishes later."

Marlon raises an eyebrow at me, then squeezes my hand tightly as we walk to our little living room and settle on the couch. I lean into his body, relishing how safe I feel with him. My love for him goes deeper than anything I thought was possible to experience. After so many years of being on my own, I had to learn how to share my life with someone.

But being with Marlon is the greatest thing I've experienced in my life. Until today. I thought my hope and joy for the future, after Marlon and I found each other and fell in love, was immense, but that has nothing compared to the news I have for him tonight.

"What's on your mind?" Marlon runs a hand through my hair and pleasure shivers over my skin. You'd think that I'd be used to all his touches, but they still give me a thrill each and every time – and I hope the thrill never fades away. Every moment with Marlon is a joy, even when we argue.

"I've been thinking about where to go next. I have something different in mind, but I think you'll like it."

"Oh, and what devious plan do you have, Angel?" Marlon grins and joy spikes through me. I giggle and squirm as his fingers drop to my waist and tickle me.

"Well," I take Marlon's hand in mine and lower it to my stomach, "I think we should go home. Maybe not to Los Angeles, but maybe someplace close, but smaller and quieter. Someplace where we could settle for a while, to raise our family."

Marlon's breath hitches and his eyes widen. We've talked about and agreed to have kids, but we never discussed when we would or where we would.

"You're…"

"Solano confirmed it today. He did an ultrasound. I've suspected for a couple of weeks now. There's a little bean inside me."

"Oh, Angel." Marlon's face softens and his eyes fill with tears as he kisses me. He moves his body so he's kneeling in front of me, then he kisses my stomach and hugs me tightly. The depth and rawness of his reaction

PROTECTED BY THE HITMAN

shakes me to my core and, once again, I know that choosing him was the right decision.

Even after all the time we've spent together, I still get surprised at the soft side of my husband. It's like after a lifetime of having to hide his feelings, he lets himself feel all of them when he's with me. He still has a tough side and doesn't hesitate to do whatever is necessary as the camp's Head of Security, but...he shares a vulnerability with me that fills my heart. He shows me his humanity and reaffirms it each and every day.

"Will you feel comfortable if we go back to the L.A. area? You know Rogue is going to try to bring you back in." I smooth Marlon's hair as he tenderly kisses my stomach, his hands stroking my body. My soul fills with even more love as I think of how we're building a family.

"He can try." Marlon's voice is gruff. "I'm not changing my mind and he knows it."

Rogue protested, loudly, when Marlon said he was leaving Ruthless, but he *did* back Marlon and give him some contacts for setting up his security business. Rogue is a no-nonsense son of a bitch, but even he has a glimmer of a heart. He says he only cares about money and his art, but he cares about his men, too.

"I appreciate that." It took longer than I want to admit, getting used to what he did for Rogue, but the knowledge that all their targets were men who had richly earned their fate...that helped me to accept Marlon's past as a hitman. I'm still not okay with murder, but I'm less okay with drug dealers and so I've made my peace with Marlon's past.

On an even deeper level, with this baby in my stomach, we'll be even more bound than ever. I put my fingers on the wedding ring around my neck, the halo that hangs over my heart when I'm at work, the smallest symbol of love between Marlon and me.

"I'll do anything for you, Angel. Anything." Marlon kisses me and I nearly start crying from the hormone surge that hits me.

"Even change diapers at three in the morning?" I tease, running my fingers through Marlon's blond hair and stroking his neck.

"Especially change diapers in the middle of the night." His smile reminds me of how perfect we are together. There's nothing we wouldn't do for each other…or our growing baby. "I love you, Angel."

"I love you, too."

ALSO BY LANA LOVE

Thank you so much for reading Protected by the Hitman! If you enjoyed this book, please leave a review!

Sign up for my newsletter! Subscribers get updates on books and sales, plus exclusive bonus content!

http://eepurl.com/dh59Xr

Also by Lana Love

HIS CURVY BEAUTY

The unputdownable series

https://www.amazon.com/dp/B07ZSF3TW9

For even more books, visit my Amazon author page at:

https://www.amazon.com/Lana-Love/e/B078KKRB1T/

WANT MORE HITMAN ROMANCE?

Catch up on the full Men of Ruthless Corp. series!

https://www.amazon.com/gp/product/B093SPL95N